TEAMWORK

Investigating Life Skills Success

Diane Lindsey Reeves with Connie Hansen

Illustrations by Ruth Bennett

Published in the United States of America by Cherry Lake Publishing Group
Ann Arbor, Michigan
www.cherrylakepublishing.com

Created and produced by Bright Futures Press
www.brightfuturespress.com

Reading Advisor: Marla Conn, MS, Ed., Literacy specialist, Read-Ability, Inc.
Illustrator: Ruth Bennett
Cover and Page Designer: Kathy Heming
Design Elements: © mijatmijatovic/Shutterstock.com; © GoodStudio/Shutterstock.com;
 © Denis Cristo/Shutterstock.com; © Lorelyn Medina/Shutterstock.com; © Yaroshenko Olena/
 Shutterstock.com; © rangsan paidaen/Shutterstock.com

Copyright ©2021 by Cherry Lake Publishing Group
All rights reserved. No part of this book may be reproduced or utilized in any form or by any means without written permission from the publisher.

Cherry Lake Press is an imprint of Cherry Lake Publishing Group.

Library of Congress Cataloging-in-Publication Data has been filed and is available at catalog.loc.gov

Cherry Lake Publishing Group would like to acknowledge the work of the Partnership for 21st Century Learning, a Network of Battelle for Kids. Please visit http://www.battelleforkids.org/networks/p21 for more information.

Printed in the United States of America
Corporate Graphics

TABLE OF CONTENTS

**What Are Soft Skills and
   Why Do I Need Them?** 4

Chapter 1 Soft Skill #1: Collaboration 6

Chapter 2 Soft Skill #2: Conflict Resolution . . . 12

Chapter 3 Soft Skill #3: Diversity 18

Chapter 4 Soft Skill #4: Empathy 24

Teamwork Quiz 30

Glossary 31

Index 32

About the Authors 32

About the Illustrator 32

What Are Soft Skills and

Skills are needed to succeed at any job you can imagine. Different jobs require different skills. Professional baseball players need good batting and catching skills. Brain surgeons need steady hands and lots of practice with a scalpel. These are examples of **hard skills** necessary to do specific jobs.

Everyone needs "**soft skills**" to succeed in life. Soft skills get personal. They are about how you behave and treat people. Soft skills are the skills you need to be the very best *you* at home, work, and school.

"Sounds good," you say. "But I don't have a job. Why do I need to worry about soft skills?"

Ahh, but you do have a job. In fact, you have a very important job. You are a student, and your job is to learn as much as you can. Learning soft skills makes you a better student now. It also gets you ready to succeed in any career you choose later.

Teamwork happens when people work together to achieve a common goal or purpose. Teamwork can be as simple as several runners winning a relay race. It can also be as complex as several nations working together toward world peace. Simple or complex, the idea behind teamwork is that results are better when the work is shared.

In this book, you get to be a soft skills **sleuth**. You will track down clues about what good (and not so good!) teamwork looks like. You will **investigate** four soft skills needed on every team:

- **Collaboration**
- **Conflict Resolution**
- **Diversity**
- **Empathy**

Why Do I Need Them?

HOW TO USE THIS BOOK

Here's how you can be a soft skills sleuth. In each chapter:

 Gather the facts. Read the description about the soft skill.

 Read the case file. Check out a situation where soft skills are needed.

 Investigate the case. Look for clues showing soft skills *successes* and soft skills *mistakes*. Keep track of the clues on a blank sheet of paper.

 Crack the case. Did you spot all the clues?

SOFT SKILL #1

Collaboration is teamwork in action. It is a process where two or more people work together to make something happen. It works best when everyone shares their unique talents, skills, and ideas to reach a goal.

One of the best examples of collaboration is a fire bucket brigade. In the days before fancy fire trucks, people fought fires with buckets of water. One person running back and forth with a bucket of water wouldn't do much good. When neighbors brought their buckets and joined in, it made a big difference. These buckets were passed person to person from the water source to the fire. Collaboration made putting the fire out quickly much more likely.

The saying that "many hands make light work" describes the best part of collaboration. Say you have a big research project for school. If you do all the work yourself, you have to come up with an idea and dig for information. Then you have to organize the information and write a report. You have to think up ways to share the information in interesting ways. Then you have to give a presentation in front of the class. Whew! It would take forever to do all this by yourself. It's a different story if you collaborate with a team.

Collaboration works best when all team members do their part. That means everyone brings their "A" game! You add your **perspective** to the project. Everyone else adds theirs. Collaboration means less work with better results

Collaboration
How-Tos

- Work toward the same goal.
- Consider every idea.
- Pull your weight in projects.
- Keep a positive attitude.
- Ask for advice when you need it.

"Be part of the solution, not part of the problem."
—Stephen Covey

SOFT SKILLS SLEUTHS: Investigating Life Skills Success

COLLABORATION

SOFT SKILLS CASE #1: COLLABORATION

The theater club is preparing for the spring play. There is still lots to do before opening day. There are lines to learn, scenery to paint, and costumes to organize. It will take plenty of collaboration to get everything done in time.

Turn the page to take a peek backstage. Is everyone following the collaboration script?

DO: Investigate collaboration successes and mistakes!

DO NOT: Write in this book!

THE SHOW MUST GO ON

TEAMWORK: COLLABORATION

COLLABORATION

Collaboration counts on teams working together. Is this team getting the job done? Where do you see collaboration in action?

Did you **find** all the *successes* and **MISTAKES**?

Start here!

Success!
This one or that one? Asking for advice is a good idea.

Mistake.
Does that costume really belong in the trash?

Success!
Painting together gets the scenes done.

Mistake.
Don't mess with your team's success.

10 SOFT SKILLS SLEUTHS: Investigating Life Skills Success

···▶ **CASE NOTES**

Can your team count on you?

Mistake.
Working against, instead of with, each other.

Did you find them all?

Mistake.
You can fuss about who's right or you can fix the bench.

Success!
Sometimes two heads (and a tree) are better than one.

Mistake.
A little help would lighten the costume load.

Mistake.
Just sitting around accomplishes nothing.

TEAMWORK: COLLABORATION

SOFT SKILL #2

You want to go to the beach for vacation. Your brother wants to go to the mountains. And your parents would rather stick close to home for a quiet **staycation**. Everyone has strong opinions about why their idea is best. No one wants to give in.

Welcome to a family conflict in need of a resolution! **Conflict resolution** is a way for two or more people to find a peaceful solution to a disagreement among them. The goal of conflict resolution is to come up with a **compromise** that everyone can agree to. A compromise is a solution where no one gets everything they want but everyone gets something they want.

For instance, your family might agree to sleep at home. But, instead of a totally quiet week, they agree to make regular trips to a water park and a nature center. This way, you get time in the water. Your brother gets plenty of time hiking the trails. And your parents get to save money on hotels. Your family reached a **consensus**, or agreement, that made everyone happy.

Conflict resolution is all about **give-and-take**. Conflict resolution only works when everyone gets a say. That's why listening to each other is the first big step in resolving any conflict. That's how you find common ground and share different perspectives, or viewpoints. It's teamwork at its best!

Resolve to Solve Conflict

- Stay cool, calm, and collected.
- Avoid bullying others to get your way.
- Listen to all sides of the story.
- Brainstorm different solutions.
- Find a solution that works for everyone.
- Respect a fair decision.

"It is amazing what you can accomplish if you do not care who gets the credit."
—Harry S. Truman

SOFT SKILLS SLEUTHS: Investigating Life Skills Success

CONFLICT RESOLUTION

SOFT SKILLS CASE #2: CONFLICT RESOLUTION

It's the championship game between the Tigers and the Grasshoppers. The score is tight, tensions are high, and . . . oh no! The referee called a foul! One team clearly agrees with the call. The other team absolutely does not. How can they resolve this conflict without losing their cool.?

Turn the page and find out!

DO: Investigate conflict resolution successes and mistakes!

DO NOT: Write in this book!

TEAMWORK: CONFLICT RESOLUTION

CONFLICT RESOLUTION WINS THE GAME

CONFLICT RESOLUTION

The stakes are high. Everyone has their own ideas about what to do. What is the fair way to resolve this conflict?

Did you find all the successes and MISTAKES?

Start here!

Mistake. Picking on the other team's players.

Success! Calmly explaining your point of view.

Success! Accepting the referee's decision.

Mistake. Insulting the other team.

SOFT SKILLS SLEUTHS: Investigating Life Skills Success

CASE NOTES

Are your conflict resolution skills winning the game?

Success! Asking for advice.

Did you find them all?

Mistake. Yelling at the referee.

Success! Agreeing to disagree.

Mistake. Stirring up trouble in the bleachers.

Mistake. Can't we all just get along?

TEAMWORK: CONFLICT RESOLUTION

SOFT SKILL #3

People are different ages, races, and genders. They speak different languages and have different religious beliefs. Their abilities differ. Some have lots of money. Others don't have enough. All this **diversity** makes the world an interesting—and complicated—place.

Sometimes people struggle with how to get along with those who are different from them. Hanging out with people who are just like you can seem easier or comfortable. The problem? Besides being really boring, it isn't fair to leave other people out.

Diverse teams are more creative, more productive, and much more interesting. Think about a baseball game. To win at baseball, you need strong hitters and good pitchers. You need players who can run fast and players who can catch balls in the outfield. What if you choose only good pitchers for your team? They can't hit home runs. They can't catch fly balls. They can only pitch. Baseball wouldn't be all that fun, would it? Not to mention, you'd never win a game!

The same is true for any team. Diverse teams reflect the real world. Bringing together different ideas, experiences, and skills makes teams stronger. It also makes you a better person. Everyone adds something special to a team.

Diversity means that everyone is welcome. It means that everyone counts. Showing respect to others is another way to respect yourself.

Keys to Diversity

- Treat everyone you meet with kindness and respect.
- Get to know people who are different from you.
- Speak up when you see someone being treated unfairly.
- Challenge **stereotypes** about the way certain people are "supposed" to be.

"We may have all come on different ships, but we're in the same boat now."
—Martin Luther King Jr.

DIVERSITY

SOFT SKILLS CASE #3: DIVERSITY

School is out, and several students are riding the city bus home. Every stop seems to bring more diversity aboard. There are differences in age, race, language, religion, and more.

Some students are comfortable with all the diversity. Some are not. Can you spot who's who?

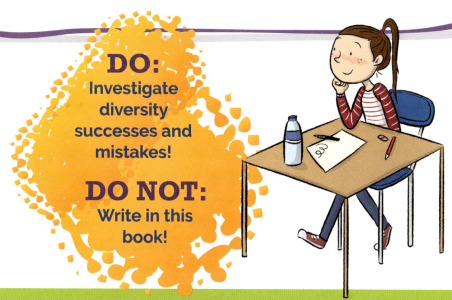

DO: Investigate diversity successes and mistakes!

DO NOT: Write in this book!

SOFT SKILLS SLEUTHS: Investigating Life Skills Success

DIVERSITY

Who is celebrating diversity?
Who is blocking its way?

Did you **find** all the **successes** and **MISTAKES**?

Start here!

Success!
It's nice when people young and old get along.

Mistake.
My language is better than yours.

Success!
Human kindness works in all religions.

Success!
Showing respect for elders.

22 SOFT SKILLS SLEUTHS: Investigating Life Skills Success

···▶ **CASE NOTES**

How diverse is your world?

Mistake. Out of my way, kid.

Success! Play another song!

Did you find them all?

Mistake. I'll stick to my own playlist, thank you very much.

Success! Offering help to someone in need.

Mistake. Will that baby ever be quiet?!?

TEAMWORK: DIVERSITY

SOFT SKILL #4

Suppose a boy in your class comes to school in dirty, ragged clothes. He always seems a bit tired and never finishes his homework. At first, you may wonder why this kid doesn't get his act together. Then you find out that his family lost their home in a fire. They are homeless and struggling to pay for things they need.

At first, you may feel sorry for him. Feeling sorry *for* someone is called **sympathy**. But if you can imagine how awful it must be to not have a home, you are feeling **empathy** *with* that person. Empathy is the ability to understand and share the feelings of another person.

Empathy means you can put yourself in the other person's shoes. You understand how difficult it must be to get a good night's rest. You can picture what it must be like to not have a place to take hot showers and clean your clothes. You realize that it must be tough to find a quiet place to do homework. In a way, empathy is the ability to feel someone else's pain and want to make things better.

Showing empathy means more than feeling sorry about a bad situation. Many times, there won't be much you can do to solve the other person's problem. You can certainly offer to help whenever possible. But listening, being a friend, and showing kindness can make a big difference too.

Showing Empathy Means

- Using your imagination to understand how the other person is feeling.
- Being a good listener when someone explains their problems.
- Treating people the way they need to be treated.

"I've learned that people will forget what you said, people will forget what you did, but people will never forget how you made them feel."
—Maya Angelou

EMPATHY

SOFT SKILLS CASE #4: EMPATHY

It's all fun and games at the rock-climbing wall until Jason gets hurt. Look at the scene on the next page. Thank goodness there is plenty of empathy on hand. Some students seem to know just what to do to help Jason feel better.

But take a closer look and you may see something else. Some students don't seem to care at all. Others are making a bad situation worse. How are some students showing a lack of empathy?

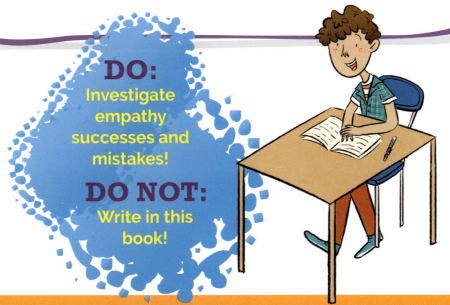

DO: Investigate empathy successes and mistakes!

DO NOT: Write in this book!

TEAMWORK: EMPATHY

EMPATHY

Can you tell the difference between sympathy, empathy, and not caring at all?

Did you **find** all the *successes* and **MISTAKES**?

Start here!

Mistake.
Hey, look at me! I am king of the rock!

Mistake.
Making fun of someone for falling.

Success!
Offering comfort when someone is in pain.

Mistake.
Ignoring someone who needs help.

···▶ **CASE NOTES**

Can you share the feelings of a friend in need?

Success! Asking an adult for help.

Success! Running for the first aid kit.

Did you find them all?

Mistake. Maybe if I just stand here and worry, Jason will feel better.

Success! Giving a friend a helping hand.

Mistake. Taking embarrassing pictures.

TEAMWORK: EMPATHY

WHAT HAVE YOU Learned?

TEAMWORK QUIZ

Question 1:
_____ is the process of working together to get something done.

Question 2:
Adding the _____ of others lets you see a situation in a different way.

Question 3:
In a _____ everyone gets something they want.

Question 4:
To reach an agreement means to come to a _____.

Question 5:
Celebrating _____ means accepting people who are different from us.

Question 6:
Diversity means that _____ matters.

Question 7:
Feeling sorry for someone who is very ill is an example of _____.

Question 8:
_____ is the ability to understand and share the feelings of someone else.

30 SOFT SKILLS SLEUTHS: Investigating Life Skills Success

ANSWERS

1. *Collaboration*
2. *perspective*
3. *compromise*
4. *consensus*
5. *diversity*
6. *everyone or all people*
7. *sympathy*
8. *Empathy*

Teamwork soft skills start here!

GLOSSARY

collaboration (kuh-lab-uh-RAY-shuhn) the process of working together to do something

compromise (KAHM-pruh-mize) an agreement about something that is not exactly what you wanted, in order to satisfy the requests of other people

conflict resolution (KAHN-flikt rez-uh-LOO-shuhn) a process that two or more people use to find a peaceful solution to a dispute

consensus (kuhn-SEN-suhs) agreement that is shared by all the people in a group

diversity (dih-VUR-sih-tee) everything that makes people different from each other

empathy (EM-puh-thee) the ability to understand and share the feelings of a person who is suffering

give-and-take (GIV AND TAYK) offering ideas and letting go of other ideas to try and reach agreement

hard skills (HAHRD SKILZ) specific skills needed to do a specific job

investigate (in-VES-tih-gate) to gather information or clues about something

perspective (pur-SPEK-tiv) a particular attitude or way of looking at something

sleuth (SLOOTH) a detective, or person who is good at finding facts and clues

soft skills (SAWFT SKILZ) behaviors and personality traits people use every day to succeed in life

staycation (stay-KAY-shuhn) a vacation that takes place at home and involves doing leisure activities that are within easy driving distance

stereotypes (STER-ee-oh-tipes) widely held but overly simple ideas, opinions, or images of a person, group, or thing

sympathy (SIM-puh-thee) feelings of pity and sorrow for someone else's misfortune

INDEX

Angelou, Maya, 25
compromise, 12
consensus, 12
Covey, Stephen, 6
empathy, 24
give-and-take, 12
King Jr., Martin Luther, 18
perspective, 12
stereotypes, 18
sympathy, 24
Truman, Harry S., 12

ABOUT THE AUTHORS

Diane Lindsey Reeves likes to write books that help students figure out what they want to be when they grow up. She mostly lives in Washington, D.C., but spends as much time as she can in North Carolina and South Carolina with her grandkids.

Connie Hansen spent 25 years teaching college students about successful life skills. She lives in Lynchburg, Virginia where her favorite thing to do is play with her grandchildren. Her happy place is the beach!

ABOUT THE ILLUSTRATOR

Ruth Bennett lives in a small country village in the heart of Norfolk, England, with her two cats, Queen Elizabeth and Queen Victoria. She loves petting dogs, watching movies, and drawing, of course!